Perry, Robert L.
Artificial Intelligence

DATE DUE

DEC 2			

Artificial Intelligence

Robert L. Perry

Watts LIBRARY

Franklin Watts
A Division of Grolier Publishing
New York • London • Hong Kong • Sydney
Danbury, Connecticut

To Tressa L. Dolbeare, my stepdaughter, for her passionate commitment to all living—not artificial—creatures

My special thanks to James P. Hogan, noted science fiction writer and author of an excellent history of artificial intelligence, *Mind Matters: Exploring the World of Artificial Intelligence*. I also sincerely appreciate the help of Ann Griffith at Applied AI Systems, Inc. for her information on biorobots and artificial life. And I wish to thank Mark Friedman, my executive editor, for allowing me to develop this series. Last, but not least, I thank the best teacher I know, my wife Marilyn L. Perry, for her constant support and timely advice.

Note to readers: Definitions for words in **bold** can be found in the Glossary at the back of this book.

Photographs ©: 3Com Corporation/Palm Computing, Inc.: 20; Archive Photos: 30, 31 (Toshiyuki Aizawa/Reuters); Daemmrich Photography: 17; Ken Lax Photography: 37; Liaison Agency, Inc.: 24 (AW & ST), 3 bottom, 10 (Jeff Christensen), 39, 40, 42; Massachusetts Institute of Technology: 3 top, 22 (Donna Coveney/MIT); Medichrome/The Stock Shop: 46 (Orin Cassill), 48 (Tom Tracy); Omni-Photo Communications: 28, 29 (Lea); Photo Researchers: 9 (Science Photo Library); PhotoEdit: 21 (Bill Aron), 7 (Spencer Grant), 14; Photofest: 4, 6; Robert Llewellyn: cover; Sony Electronics Inc.: 41; Stock Boston: 12 (Charles Gupton), 16, 26, 27 (Richard Pasley); Superstock, Inc.: 11; Switzer Corporation: 34; The Image Works: 32 (Fujifotos), 18, 19 (David Lassman).

Visit Franklin Watts on the Internet at: http://publishing.grolier.com

Library of Congress Cataloging-in-Publication Data

Perry, Robert L. (Robert Louis), 1950-
Artificial Intelligence/by Robert L. Perry
p. cm. — (Watts Library)
Includes bibliographical references and index.
Summary : Describes different types of artificial intelligence from heuristic to case-based reasoning and beyond, explores robotics, softbots, and games, and defines how AI relates to computers and humans.
ISBN: 0-531-11757-X
1. Artificial intelligence--Juvenile literature. [1. Artificial intelligence.] I. Title. II.Series.
Q335.4.P47 2000
006.3-dc21

99-088785

GROLIER PUBLISHING

Printed in the United States of America.
1 2 3 4 5 6 7 8 9 10 R 09 08 07 06 05 04 03 02 01 00

Contents

The movie Star Wars *featured humanlike robots called R2D2 and C3P0.*

Chapter One

What Is Artificial Intelligence?

For more than 2,500 years, humans have dreamed of creating machines that could think and do the same things that people do. The dream is as old as the ancient Greek myths and as new as our modern science fiction books and movies. For example, in the movie *Star Wars*, R2D2 and C3P0 are thinking, feeling, knowing **robots** in a galactic civilization where

Commander Data, featured on the TV show Star Trek: The Next Generation, *seems to be a human, but he's an android.*

Could Your Neighbor Be an Android?

An android is a mobile robot that usually looks and acts like a human.

robots are as common as automobiles are today.

In all of the *Star Trek* television series and movies, highly intelligent computers that act like humans control most of the critical functions of the starships. During one episode of *Star Trek: The Next Generation* TV series, a trial was held to determine whether Commander Data, an android, was a machine that people could turn on and off at will, or if he was a knowing being with freedom and individual rights. Fortunately for Commander Data, the judge ruled that he was a new life form, and was entitled to the same rights as every other "intelligent" life form in the universe.

The Startling Reality

The reality of "intelligent" machines or artificial life forms may be more surprising than you think. Intelligent machines

A police robot handles a live bomb by using a remote control device.

already affect your life, and they exist everywhere in a number of forms. Did you know that some part of almost every automobile in the world is made by an assembly robot? Likewise, the police use robots to defuse bombs. The military uses flying robots and robotic vehicles to spy on the enemy. The NASA shuttle has a robotic arm to handle payloads. When

The Rise of the Robot

The word robot comes from a 1921 play by Czech playwright Karel Capek. It was derived from a Czech word *robota*, which means, "forced labor." But it was science fiction author Isaac Asimov who first popularized the idea of the robot in his 1950 novel, *I, Robot.*

you surf the Internet with a search engine, "intelligent" software called a **softbot** (software robot) may find the information you want. If you ever play chess, checkers, poker, backgammon, and adventure games against a computer, you may be playing against "intelligent" software.

What Is Artificial Intelligence?

Artificial intelligence (commonly abbreviated as "AI") is everywhere; however, no one has even come close to duplicating *human* intelligence. That's because no one has figured out yet how the human brain actually works. In fact, people can't even agree on a definition of intelligence, much less come to terms with a definition of artificial intelligence.

"Artificial" means that something is made by humans rather than "natural," or occurring through biological, chemical, or physical processes. The definition of intelligence includes these capabilities:

- To learn or understand from experience
- To gain and retain new knowledge
- To change behavior to achieve goals
- To use reason and logic to make decisions and solve problems
- To use mental processes to carry out tasks

Building a machine that can use some or all of these capabilities should mean that you had created artificial intelligence. Or does it?

Enter the Turing Test

In 1950, Alan M. Turing, a British mathematician, developed the Turing Test for artificial intelligence. Could a machine deceive an interrogator into thinking that it was human? In the test, the examiner questioned two things, or entities, that it could not see. One was a person, and the other was a machine. The examiner asked a series of questions in a dialogue with either the machine or the person (he didn't know which one) until he determined which entity was the machine.

Alan M. Turing was a brilliant mathematician who invented a test for artificial intelligence. No machine has ever met the requirements of his test.

Turing's goal was to find a machine that could use a variety of experiences and knowledge, speak in a natural language, build on what it knew, and learn from its answers during the test. That is a tall order, and no machine or computer has ever come close to meeting his test.

Since 1956, AI researchers have pursued two main directions for AI research:

- An AI machine should show all-purpose, human-level intelligence.
- An AI machine should carry out definite tasks in a way that would be considered "intelligent" if humans did those tasks.

These directions have taken AI research into very different fields: robotics, handwriting and voice recognition, speech synthesis, **natural language** machines, **machine vision,** expert systems, **fuzzy logic** systems, neural networks, and more.

Computers Don't Have Feelings

Researchers have already created many machines and programs that can mimic, or act like, some aspects of human thinking. For example, computers have been able to beat amateur game players for several years. In 1997, Deep Blue, a very powerful, dedicated chess computer made by IBM, beat a reigning human world champion, Garry Kasparov, for the first time, even though Kasparov had beaten a less sophisticated computer the year before.

World champion chess player, Garry Kasparov, attempts to defeat the IBM supercomputer called Deep Blue.

However, no one has created any "thing" that can *feel* or *know* (be conscious of) life. To be conscious is to be aware of

your existence as a thinking being and know what you are doing and why you are doing it.

No computer can yet say, "I think, therefore I am," and understand what that means. No computer can love another computer or a person. No computer can hurt someone else's feelings and apologize and feel badly for its mistake. No computer can look up at night at a sky full of stars and feel awe.

There is a clear difference between "intelligence" and "consciousness." The top researchers say that the complexities of the human brain make it highly unlikely that a computer or a machine will be able to be aware or conscious of its own existence for many years to come—if ever.

In 1956, Robby the robot, pictured in the movie The Forbidden Planet, *was the way we pictured future robots would look.*

Some researchers thought that the human brain could be duplicated by a series of mathematical formulas, but so far that hasn't worked.

Chapter Two

Types of Artificial Intelligence

During the 1950s, the study of artificial intelligence (AI) was divided into two schools of thought: "Strong AI" and "Weak AI." Strong AI followers thought that all human thinking was only a series of algorithms (mathematical rules). They believed it would be possible to duplicate the processes of the human brain in computers—to create a self-aware robot that

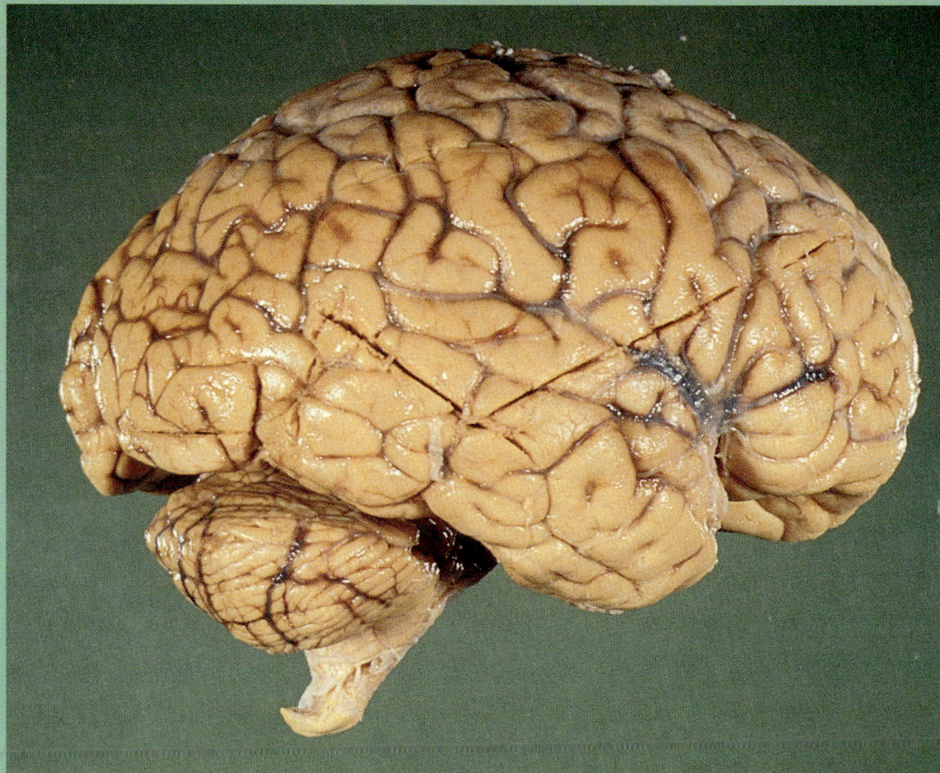

The Fantastic Human Brain

The human brain is estimated to have 100 *billion* neurons, separate microscopic organic processors, in it. Each neuron has connections to at least several thousand other connections, or synapses. The average human brain may have more than 100 *trillion* connections that send signals back and forth constantly.

could think and feel like a human, as well as react like a human.

However, Weak AI followers believed that the human mind was unique and that computers would be able only to simulate some aspects of the way people think. They thought that because the living human brain evolved over three billion years, it was too unique for people to fully understand, much less reproduce.

So far, Weak AI followers have been proven to be correct because almost all practical AI developments have been limited to specific uses. Although some general purpose AI computers have been developed, none has had the intelligence of even an insect.

Types of AI

AI can be divided into three major categories: heuristic, or rules-based AI, pattern recognition, and natural learning.

Heuristics is the study and use of the rules by which processes work. For example, IBM's Deep Blue chess computer defeated Kasparov because it had been programmed to know all the moves, variations, and consequences of those moves for playing chess. With hundreds of microprocessors, it searched through tens of thousands of possible moves and their consequences each second.

However, this is not true for human thinking. If Kasparov had to do the same thing, he could never have made a move. Rather, he used his experience, knowledge, judgment, and intuition to isolate a few moves and make the best choices. To win, Deep Blue defeated Kasparov by avoiding human emotions, physical and mental fatigue, and stress. It did what computers do best—it kept grinding through the possible moves until it found the best one for the situation.

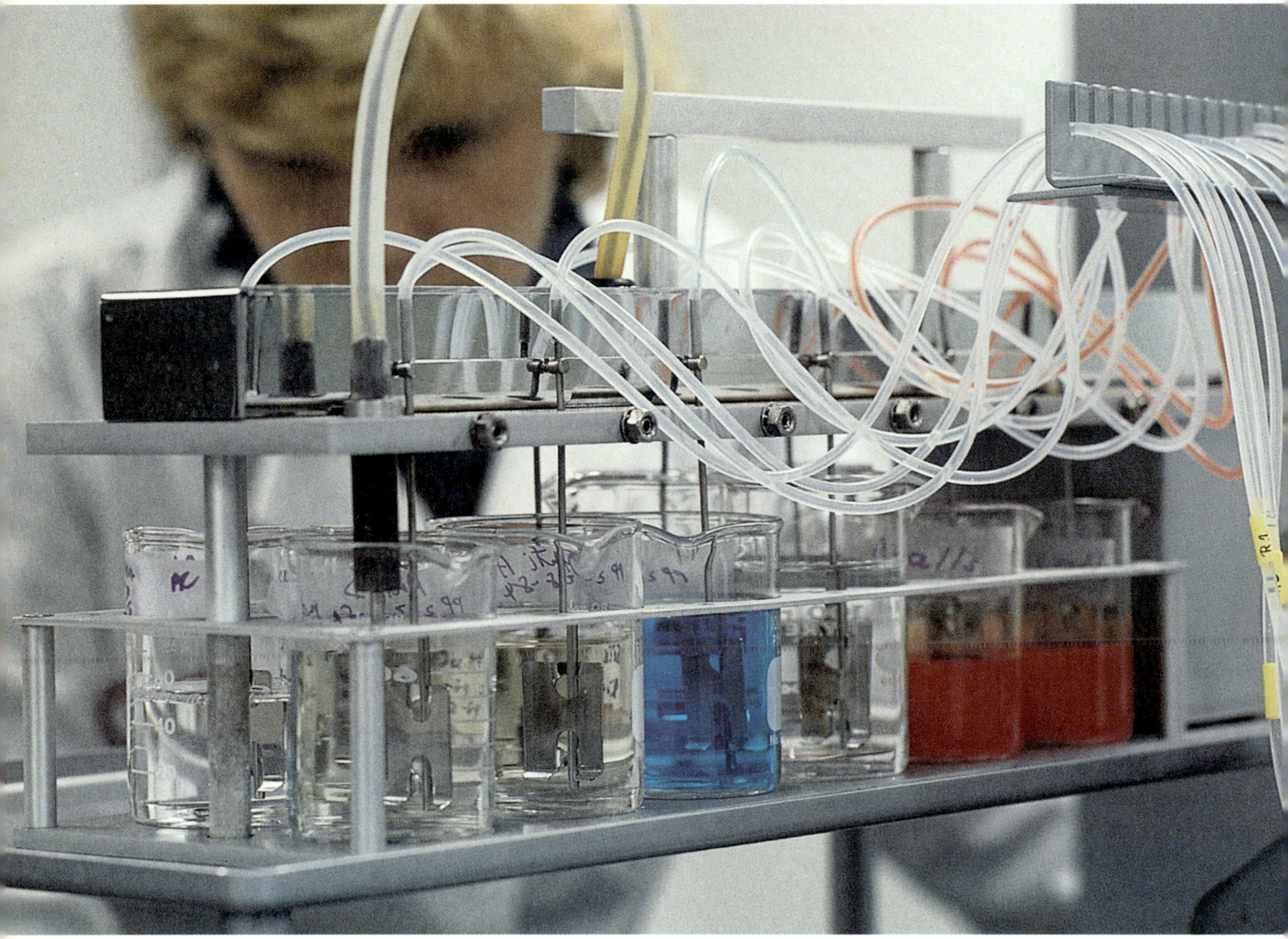

This blood analysis machine helps doctors diagnose and treat problems with the blood.

In a similar fashion, expert systems are programmed with the knowledge of experts in a field. To obtain this knowledge, programmers interview experts thoroughly to identify everything they know. Then the programmers write software that uses the experts' knowledge to solve problems. For example, the MYCIN expert system helps doctors diagnose blood infections, and it suggests tests and treatment.

Case-based Reasoning

Case-based reasoning (CBR) takes the rules approach another step. A program is given all the facts, information, and rules it needs to resolve a series of case studies. Then the program suggests a solution to the present situation, based on solutions that worked in the past.

CBR is becoming widely used in customer service and support. For example, LucasArts Entertainment, Inc., creator of *Star Wars* games, has Yoda's Help Desk at its website *http://www.lucasarts.com*. Using a series of questions in a conversational dialogue with a game player, it solves about 80 percent of the 500–1,000 problems it is given daily.

This approach enters millions of basic assumptions and rules about people and how they behave into a program. Then the program uses all those rules to learn what to do or how to respond in any given situation. For example, Doug Lenat and his team in Austin, Texas have entered more than two million rules into the CYC program. Lenat hopes to create an artificial brain that can learn the way children do—by learning new facts, gathering information,

In Texas, researcher Doug Lenat is trying to create an artificial brain with a computer.

experiencing new things, and drawing conclusions about them.

A variation on expert systems, intelligent agents (or softbots) help people, such as air traffic controllers and pilots, make decisions based on a system's "knowledge" of the rules for the situation.

Pattern Recognition

In pattern recognition, computers are programmed to understand patterns of information and then repeat, use, or respond to those patterns. This category includes several more types of AI, including handwriting and voice recognition (computers that recognize spoken words), speech synthesis (computers that "talk" or duplicate human language), and machine vision (computers that "see" or use sensors to recognize visual patterns). Many websites also use pattern recognition to track which websites you visit. Then they might choose an advertisement or create a list of similar websites for you to enhance your time on the Internet.

Artificial intelligence helps air traffic controllers manage traffic flow and schedule planes.

Handwriting and Voice Recognition

Perhaps the most popular form of AI is handwriting recognition. You can now buy such devices as Palm Pilot or Handspring's Visor. On these computers, there is an area on the screen that you can write on with a special pen (called a stylus), or you can even use your finger to write down information. Currently, these minicomputers are only used for storing addresses, notes, memos, or lists.

Among the more advanced AI technologies, **voice recognition** (VR) uses microphones, advanced rules, and pattern-

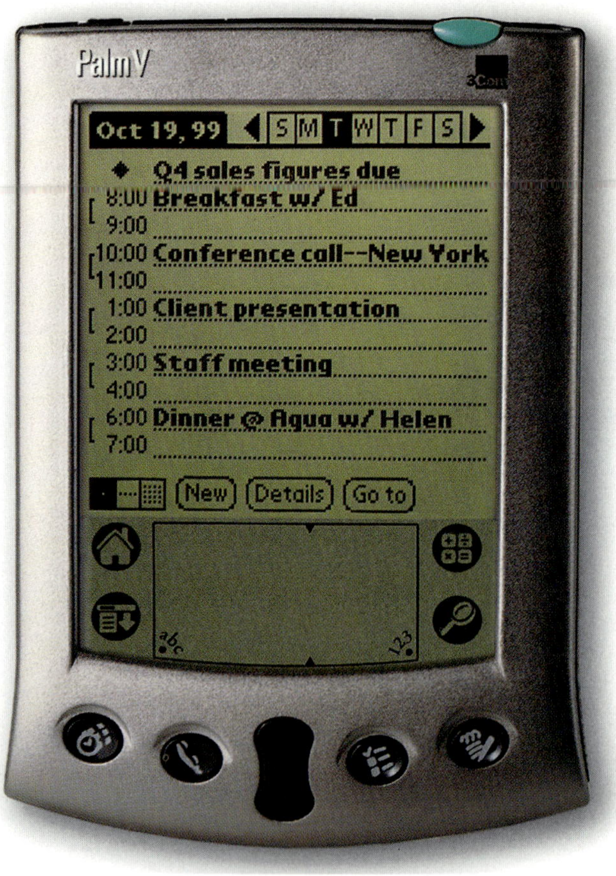

The Palm Pilot V organizer is a modern-day way to write memos and keep addresses.

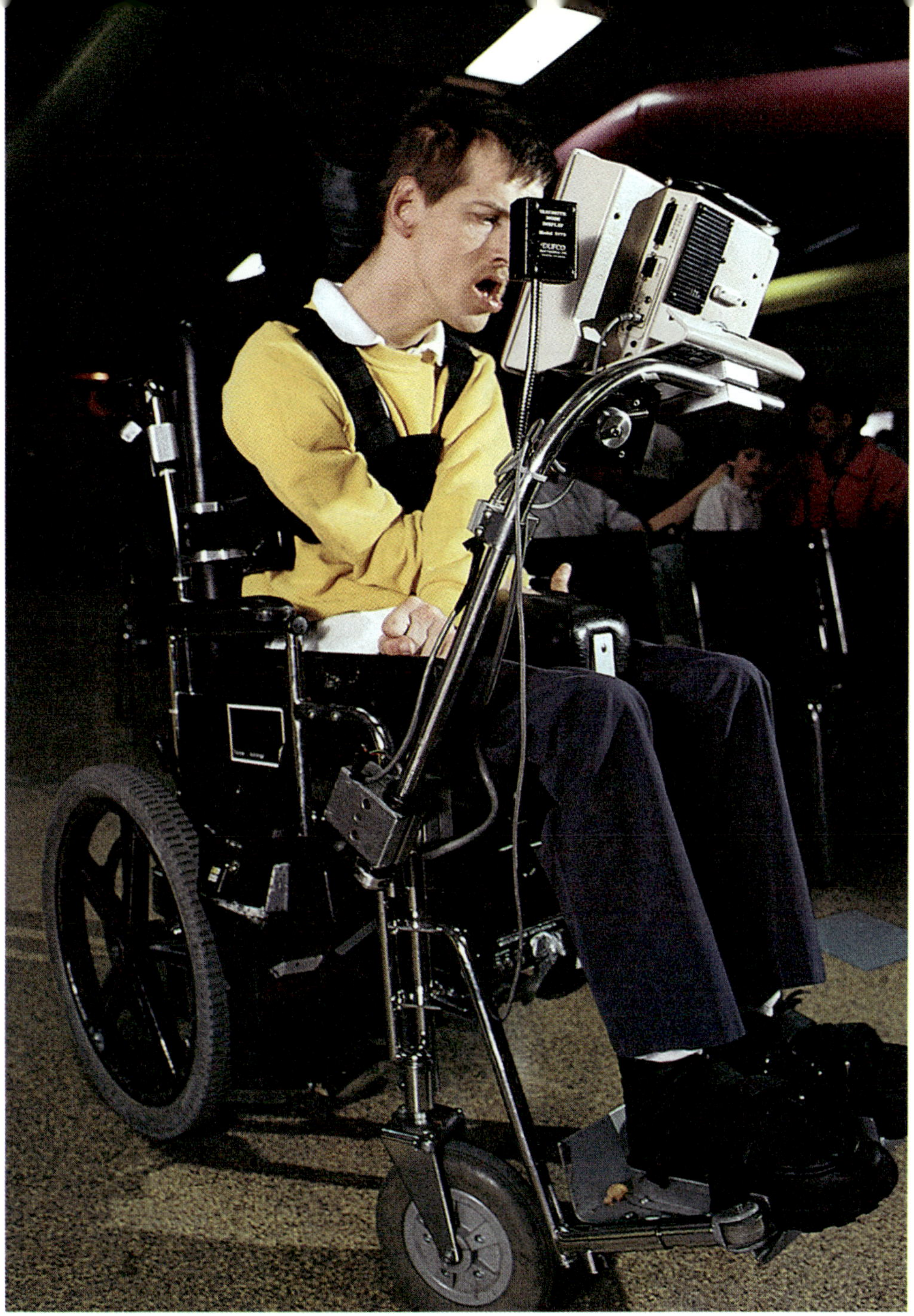

A disabled man is able to communicate, thanks to the computer that is attached to his wheelchair.

matching software and learning techniques to "learn" to recognize different voices. As VR "hears" you talk, speech synthesis software "talks" back to you. It uses the rules of

Learning from Sensory Experience

AI computers are also learning by experience through the "senses." At the Massachusetts Institute of Technology (MIT), a robot called Cog has cameras for eyes (machine vision), microphones for ears (sound and voice recognition), and robotic arms with "hands" (touch sensing). Rather than program it with a set of rules, the MIT researchers allow Cog to roam around a lab so it can learn "hand-eye" coordination and "recognize" human faces on its own.

language, grammar, and syntax to speak in a relatively normal way. The computer must be able to understand quickly and correctly—the first time—a simple sentence such as "I, too, am going to the park to play with my two cousins," or "I'm hungry, and I want to eat." The late-1990s Furby toy uses simple speech synthesis and voice recognition to make it an interactive toy.

Machine Learning

Machine vision has become common in industry today. To "see" an object, an AI machine uses a solid-state camera, microcomputer chips, and an AI program to compare the object it is looking at with an ideal image of the object, which is stored in its memory. Modern machine vision devices can also "see" in three dimensions (3-D). These machines do everything from assembling cars to cutting boards in lumber mills.

More advanced than the rules-based systems, **machine learning** programs improve their actions or "learn" in somewhat humanlike ways. The best known methods are **neural networks**, natural language systems, and fuzzy logic systems.

Neural networks improve their actions with feedback signals that tell the program to keep doing a correct action and to stop doing an incorrect action. After a number of repetitions, the signals increase the number of electrical pathways that act correctly and get rid of those that make mistakes. The network "learns" like you do when you make a mistake and then correct your mistake. Neural networks already help manage huge telephone networks and track submarines under the ocean.

The original version of natural language systems recognized only patterns of letters or statistics to identify words. The advanced version actually analyzes the structure of language, that is, sentences, meanings, and situations. This is important because words can mean different things in differ-

Flying Robot Combines AI Methods

CYPHER, a robotic helicopter built for the United States Army, uses machine vision and sensors to track people and vehicles for possible military operations. Six feet (1.83 meters) in diameter, it uses heuristic programs to take off, fly, and land by itself.

ent situations. For example, among its many meanings, the word "high" can mean height, as in twenty stories high, or above-average value, as in a high price for a new game. Now, this language system is being taught to differentiate between the various meanings of words.

A growing AI field, fuzzy logic, is based on probability, that is, the degree of likelihood that something is correct or that something is going to happen. If something is probable, that means it is more than possible, but less than certain.

As intelligent as these methods seem to make computers, they still do not come close to human intelligence. They can't tell stories and understand what they mean. They can't tell jokes or cry real tears. But they can and do perform many tasks that people find boring, difficult, or dangerous. Computers have become an indispensable part of our lives today.

An unmanned, underwater robot searches the depths of the ocean.

Chapter Three

Artificial Intelligence Today

You won't find domestic robots for sale at the department store. You won't find cars that drive themselves or robotic doctors that operate on people. However, you will find bits and pieces of practical AI applications everywhere from the Internet to your family car, and from your parents' company to the far reaches of outer space and the depths of the oceans.

Slowly, but surely, AI is becoming widely used and easily accepted. AI is becoming a tool in business and industry wherever it can do something faster, cheaper, more safely, and more accurately than people can. There are many ways in which AI is making a difference in our lives.

The best-known artificial intelligence is in robots, which already do many repetitive or dangerous tasks. Subway trains have automated drivers that prevent accidents better than people do. Robots dig dangerous mine shafts, mow fields of grass, and "sniff" for bombs, hazardous waste spills, and nuclear radiation.

"Invisible" AI

As exciting as robots are, you can't even see the most widely used business applications of AI because they are stored as computer programs. They include expert systems that architects use to plan buildings and that workers use to repair computers and copiers online. Our cities use computers to control such functions as the regulation of utilities and even our stoplights. And there are softbots searching the Internet for information or helping to sell products or give customer service.

For example, when someone applies for a credit card or loan, a softbot may review his or her application and recommend a decision long before a real person ever sees it. Or, an AI program used by an accountant may help fill out a tax return for the Internal Revenue Service.

Robots can help in everything we do, including this robotic, solar-powered lawn mower.

Virtual Humans Arrive

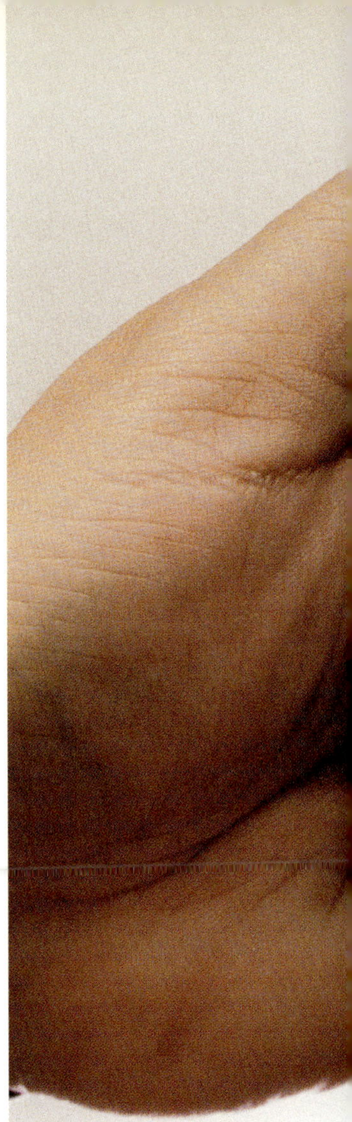

Soon, you and your family may even use an avatar, or **virtual personality,** that manages your phone calls, electronic mail, appointment schedule, and daily planner. One virtual personality called Webley already provides these services. It uses AI to understand the spoken voice, manage information, and respond in natural speech.

Jack, a virtual person developed at the University of Pennsylvania, is a 3-D software "human" that can run, walk, sit, stand, and even duck like a real person. With the virtual body of an average male, Jack is used in simulated car wrecks, building fires, airplane crashes, and even "driving" lawn mowers to improve safety

Although Jack is not going to move in with you quite yet, you may find many AI applications around your home. Your family or a relative may own a digital camera with AI software that creates a better photograph. Perhaps you or someone you know has a Furby or other virtual pet, with its own basic learning ability and personality. Many of your computer games use AI techniques for

fantastic graphics and action in sports games, role-playing adventures, and thinking games. All in all, artificial intelligence is rapidly becoming an important part of your daily life.

A digital camera is possible because of AI software.

Interesting AI Applications

The following list inludes many areas where AI touches our everyday lives.

Dangerous Environments

- Searching for oil, shipwrecks, and minerals with underwater robots
- Using robotic rovers on Mars and other planets
- Preventing disasters at oil refineries, chemical plants, and nuclear power plants
- Digging new mines to find gold, precious metals, coal, and iron

In Tokyo, Japan, this robot, owned by a power company, works on dangerous power lines so that human workers won't get hurt.

Weather Forecasting

- Giving long-range weather predictions
- Tracking serious storms, such as tornadoes and hurricanes
- Predicting earthquakes

Medicine

- Diagnosing serious illnesses
- Performing difficult, dangerous operations
- Designing better artificial joints, limbs, and organs

National Defense

- Tracking hidden submarines beneath the ocean
- Keeping the Stealth fighter hidden from enemy radar
- Monitoring millions of telephone calls

Transportation

- Preventing airplane, train, and auto crashes
- Designing better quality planes, trains, and automobiles
- Controlling and preventing traffic jams
- Engineering
- Designing machines
- Developing new materials

Can you build a toy that carries a cola?

Chapter Four

Projects and Games

You can find dozens of games, toys, and projects that use AI methods. In fact, AI will become commonplace in the toys and games of the future. This chapter lists just a few of the AI examples that already exist and gives interesting game sites on the World Wide Web. Games are well suited for AI because all of them follow clear rules. Most AI-based games use heuristic methods to learn and apply the rules when the computer plays against a human opponent.

Checkers Information Online

The American Checker Federation at *www.primenet.com/~krow* is the official website for U.S. checkers players and has links to other sites.

Backgammon Online

Backgammon Galore! (*www.bkgm.com*) is a commercial site with links to numerous websites, game sites, commercial programs, and information.

Game Sites

The Internet Gaming Zone (*www.zone.com*) offers many free board games, including backgammon, bingo, bridge, checkers, chess, cribbage, Go, hearts, reversi, and spades. It does charge fees for other games, and is owned by Microsoft.

The Softseek site (*http://softseek.com*) offers freeware (free software you can download), shareware (inexpensive software), free trials of commercial software, and demonstrations of new programs. A recent tour revealed more than 100 board games and more than 125 sports games, many of them using AI techniques.

You can play games against "intelligent" computers at many interesting and free websites. Numerous sites are available through any search engine (Yahoo, Alta Vista, Lycos, Excite, InfoSeek, and so on). The sites listed in this chapter include some board and card games with well-known AI programs.

You can study the IBM Deep Blue game that defeated human world champion Garry Kasparov at this site: *www.chess.ibm.com/meet*. Other sites for chess include chess.net ™ at *www.chess.net* and the U.S. Chess Federation at *www.uschess.org*, the official U.S. organization. You can find many chess programs through websites, on CD-ROMs at stores, through freeware and shareware sites, and at other places.

The University of Alberta at *www.cs.ualberta.ca* offers Chinook, the world championship checkers program, and numerous links to interesting sites. You can play free games against Chinook at three levels, from beginner to advanced.

You can explore the first expert backgammon program, TD-Gammon, based on a neural network by IBM, from *www.sciam.com/1998/1198intelligence/1198ginsbergbox1.html.*

Based on a Japanese board game, the Handtalk program (*www.yutopian.com*) is the most advanced AI version of the game. Find the American Go Association at *www.usgo.org*.

Scrabble is a popular game to play on the computer.

Electronic Sports

Electronic Arts (*www.easports.com*) offers these games using AI: Triple Play, Madden NFL, NHL Hockey, NBA Live, March Madness, and FIFA Soccer.

Logistello, the most advanced AI version, can be found at *www.neci.nec.com/homepages/mic*. The University of Alberta researchers have developed Loki, an advanced AI poker-playing program: *www.cs.ualberta.ca/~games/poker*. The popular word game, Scrabble, is owned by Hasbro Toys, so information about the Scrabble CD-ROM can be found at *www.hasbro scrabble.com*.

Many popular sports games have begun to include basic AI methods to make their action and characters more realistic. Be sure to check out all sports and adventure game publishers to find out how they are using AI in their games.

The Beginning of AI Toys

Tomogotchi, a virtual pet on a key chain, was first introduced in 1996 in Japan by Bandai. The toy was almost impossible to buy because Bandai didn't anticipate how popular it would be. You can feed, walk, clean up, and pet your virtual Tomogotchi pet, as well as watch it grow… and die. Since their introduction, many other companies have created new and different virtual toys.

During 1998 and 1999, two toys based on AI concepts—the cute, talking Furby and the robotic Lego® MIND STORMS™—were among the more popular toys for very different reasons. While talking, moving dolls have been around for a long time, Furby, an AI animatronic device, took the traditional doll much further. Each doll not only had a

Furby's Large Vocabulary

Furby can learn and speak a limited, yet remarkable, vocabulary of up to 800 phrases in its own "Furbish" language and English.

unique name that it responded to, but also a unique personality. It used six sensors, infrared technology, and natural language methods to learn new words and new responses when kids played with it. Rather than repeat what it said, it could change its responses and learn new ones—up to a point. For more information, check out the Furby website at *www.furby .com*.

LEGO® MINDSTORMS™ allowed you to create your own robots. LEGO® has combined its long-popular building bricks with a programmable Robotics Invention System (RIS). The system includes the RCX (Robotic Command Explorer)

Lego unveils a new "intelligent" brick.

microcomputer, CD-ROM software, two motors, two touch sensors, a light sensor, an infrared transmitter, and more than 700 bricks. You can add two RIS Expansion Modules: Extreme Creatures and Robo Sports. Visit the website (*www.legomind storms.com*) to see what creative users have built.

In 1999, Sony introduced Aibo, the first robotic dog. At $2,000 per robot, Sony sold out of these pets in four days.

Although Aibo needs to be recharged every night, you can train your robot dog to respond to your voice and do tricks. It can "see" by using infrared light. You can also purchase a memory stick that boosts Aibo's intelligence if you do not want to train it. These toys demonstrate that AI is reaching into every aspect of our lives.

You don't have to feed Aibo, but you do have to train him.

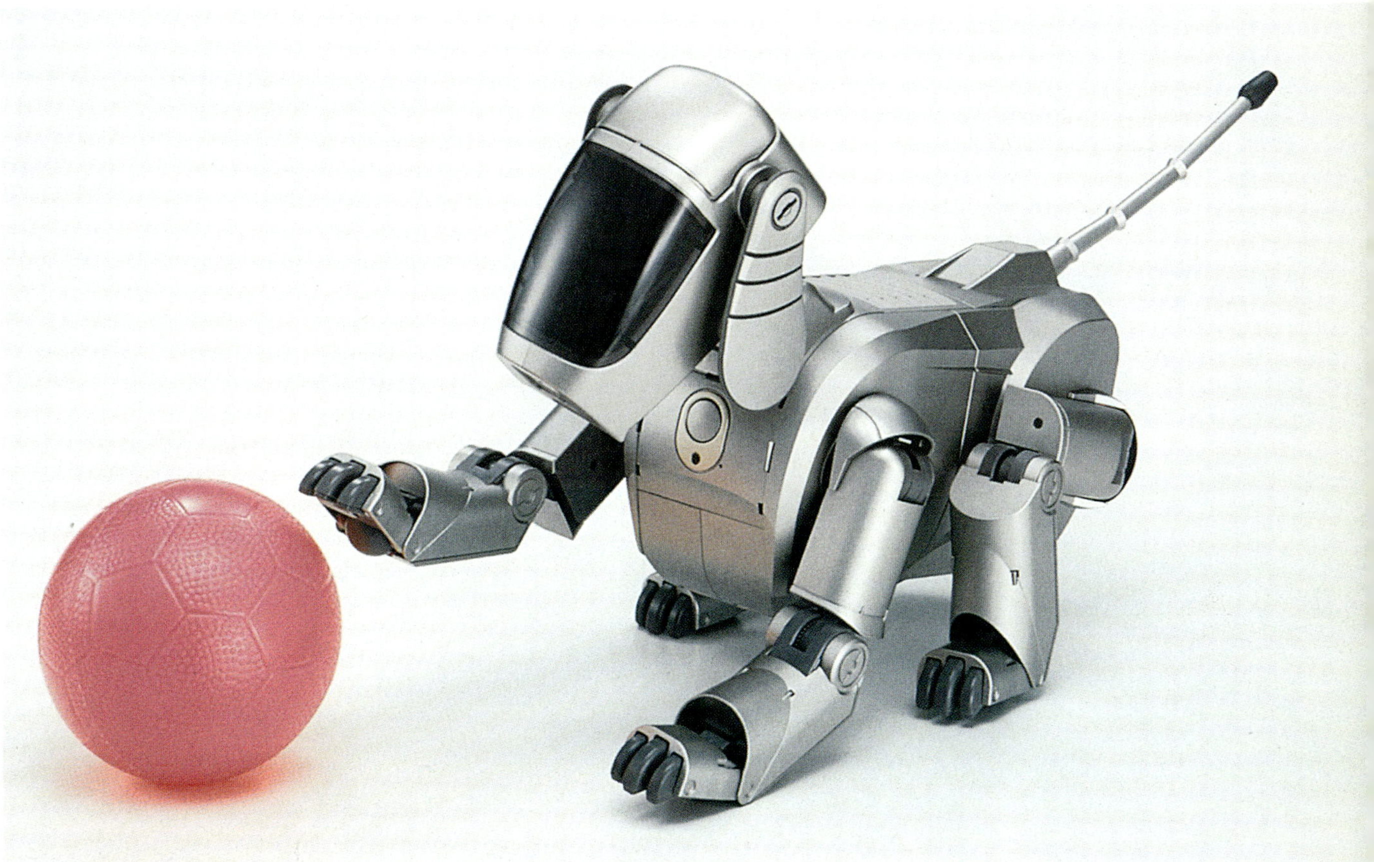

Thanks to artificial intelligence, we will be able to scan and check out our own groceries.

Chapter Five

The Future of AI

Several things seem likely to happen in the future of AI. First, bits and pieces of AI techniques and all kinds of specialized robots will become more and more useful in hundreds of ways. And, except in military applications, AI will be friendly, easy to use, and inexpensive. Second, most of us will welcome new AI technology because we will interact with pleasant, smiling faces that seem practically human on our computer screens. An advanced softbot called a **verbot** (verbal

Lots of Bots

Other types of intelligent assistants include chatterbots for telephone-based customer service and nannybots, which monitor machines, processes, and people.

robot) with a virtual personality will be programmed to recognize your voice and respond to your emotions as well as your commands.

Verbots represent the leading edge of the strong trend toward **intelligent assistants**, with programs combining voice recognition, speech synthesis, natural language, and other AI methods. In business, they can do many secretarial functions, such as answer phones, manage voice and electronic mail, send faxes, search for information, take dictation, manage schedules, arrange meetings, and more.

In fact, Virtual Personalities, Inc. (*www.vperson.com*) has already created three female Verbots™, who are extremely lifelike. Webley Systems (*www.webley.com*) already sells an intelligent assistant service with the accent of a British butler. Called Webley, the Verbot manages phone calls, e-mail, and voice mail, as well as arranging schedules.

Virtual Humans with "Emotions"

Verbots, the Furby toy, and similar animatronic toys are among the first versions of what are called virtual humans (or animals). Virtual humans, which are programmed to reflect human physical traits in simulations, are used like smart, crash-test dummies in dangerous situations and for medical research. By 2010, they could be combined with robots and become common in industry, medicine, the military, and entertainment.

These virtual humans may even appear to be able to

express their feelings or, at least, respond to your feelings with **emotional intelligence** (also called "affective computing") and common sense. Dr. Marvin Minsky, a long-time AI leader, says that people's emotions come from thousands of biochemical switches in the brain. He believes that emotions can be simulated with AI programs.

Several major research groups are developing software that can interpret the feelings behind your smiles and frowns, speech patterns, and gestures. They want the programs to recognize and respond to how you act and speak and how you express your emotions. By 2010, your computer may be able to "know" when you are happy or depressed, confused or certain, fearful or confident. It may even be able to cheer you up or give advice.

The "Emotional" Computer

In turn, your computer may have "emotions" of its own. At the very least, it may be able to know when it has a problem and tell you about it. Imagine your computer speaking to you: "Sam, I'm unhappy. I think my hard drive is about to crash."

Even more likely, the computer will call the repair shop on its own and get "cured" of its ailment without bothering you. Not only is this possible, but many companies already use remote dial-in diagnostic and repair systems to communicate with office and factory equipment. If you add some VR, synthetic speech, and AI, you've got an "emotional" machine that tells you when it feels good and when it feels bad.

In the future, computers may run our households through the use of the Internet and satellite dishes.

The secret to most of these remarkable probabilities comes from the incredible power and capacity of the Internet. Powerful AI programs will reside in thousands of host computers across the Internet, not only in the computer on your desk. Millions of intelligent agents and virtual humans could be everywhere across the Internet for thousands of common uses.

Your "Thinking" Home

In your home, basic "thinking" abilities could be built into your refrigerator, dishwasher, washer/dryer, heating/air conditioning system, security alarms, stereo system, television, home electrical system, and more. All of them would be connected to the Internet either through your telephone or cable TV, but more likely through a small satellite dish. Each home or personal appliance could be run by hundreds of processor chips that would be smart enough to know how to light your house at night, dial for help, and tell you when the house needs maintenance.

This is already possible with current technology. You can download thousands of programs, music, audio, and video files through the Internet to your computer. And Sharp Electronics already sells a system that downloads music from the web to your home audio system, storing the songs on a read-write compact disk. Using similar technology, it's relatively easy to "teach" your home appliances to do the same thing.

A Real "Incredible Journey"

If you think it's incredible that your refrigerator could tell someone it is "sick," the reason it "knows" that it is sick is even more fantastic: **microelectromechanical systems** (MEMS), also called micromachines or microscopic robots, could be roaming around inside the refrigerator's tubes and pipes, keeping track of how worn they are.

MEMS, some experts predict, are about to create the next great technological revolution. MEMS combine thousands, even hundreds of thousands, of microscopic sensors, motors, software, and AI onto silicon chips. The chips can be as small as molecules, only billionths of a meter long (nanometer).

In medicine, MEMS could make it possible for us to take "the incredible journey" through the human body. MEMS wandering through your veins could identify problems, cure diseases, and repair or replace parts of diseased organs.

In industry, inexpensive MEMS could replace expensive parts in computer hardware, auto engines, factory machines, chemical plants, and much more. They could help keep airplanes safe, warn about impending earthquakes and volcanic eruptions, and sense dangerous problems with bridges, air-

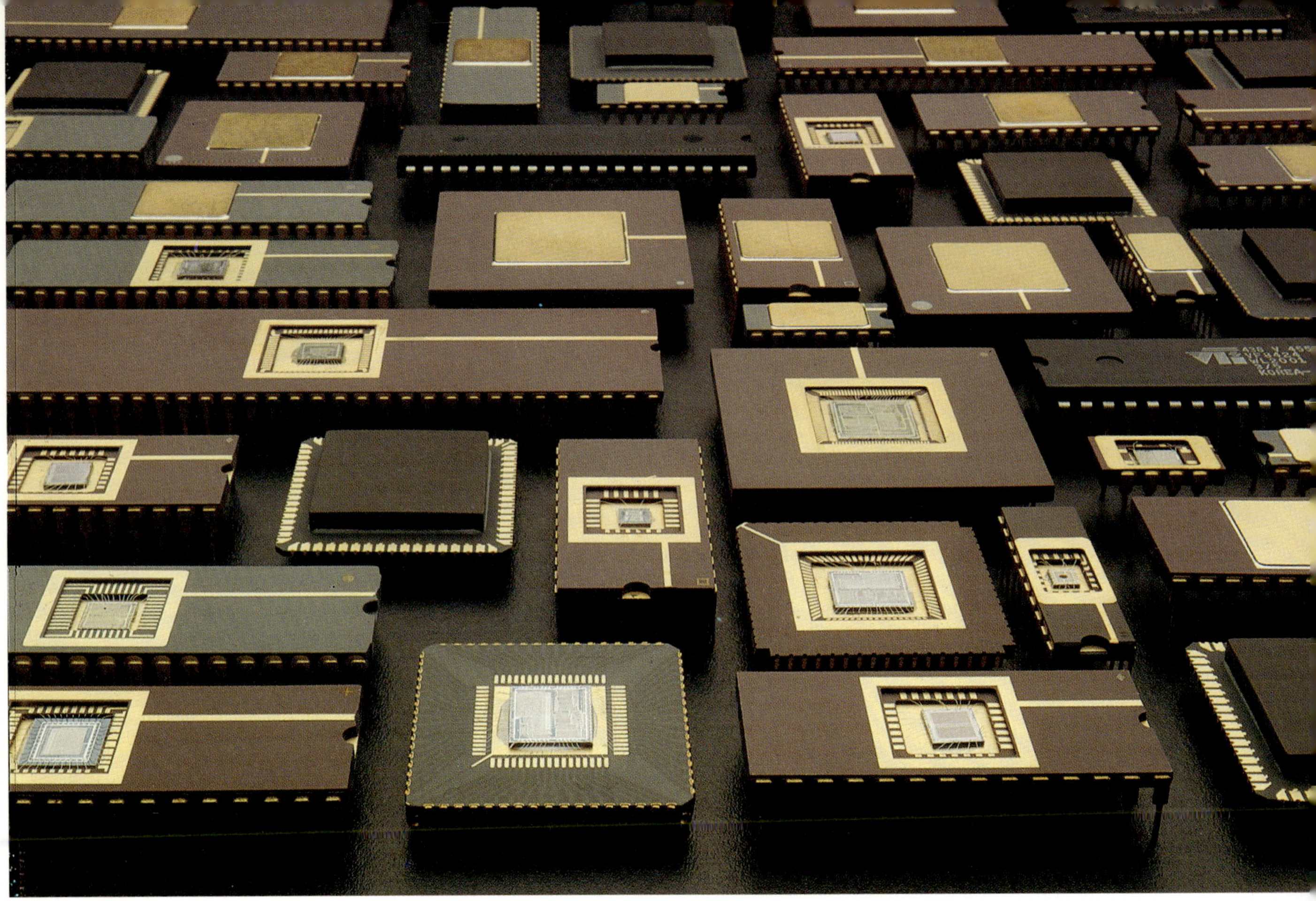

Silicon chips are at the root of our technology, and they are what makes artificial intelligence work as well as it does.

plane wings, nuclear power plants, hazardous waste dumps, chemical plants, and so on.

Linked across the Internet, these micromachines could use high-speed optical transmission (light waves) and satellite technology to create vast microscopic, yet intelligent, networks. MEMS could manage most of the next generation of telecommunications networks and reduce the cost of phone calls to almost nothing. With satellite and infrared technology, wireless MEMS could be built into every computer and embedded in the ceiling of every office, home, airplane, and more.

Artificial Life and Biorobots

As fantastic as all these new technologies are, they are still simply the beginning. Many research companies are developing **artificial life** and **biorobots**. They try to duplicate how human evolution works—but at a much faster pace—so the robots can learn and improve their tasks very quickly. Biorobots are already being tested for dozens of applications, such as exploring space, detecting land mines, exploring deep oceans, guiding an intelligent wheelchair, driving autonomous vehicles (no human driver), and even inspecting sewers.

Other researchers are developing holographic neural technology that allows one artificial "brain" cell to work thousands of times better than current neural networks. It still won't match the human brain, but it could bring us closer than ever before to a match. Artificial intelligence combined with all these new technologies can make smart computers even smarter. However, AI can and will be used for both good and evil. Fortunately, like every other technology, AI can help us live healthier, easier, more intelligent, more interesting lives—if we choose to use it that way.

Artificial Intelligence Timeline

250 BCE	Ctesibius of Alexandria, Greek inventor, builds a clepsydra, or water clock, that refills itself, moving puppets and ringing bells.
17th Century	Louis XIV's Royal Gardens at Versailles are filled with "robots" controlled by water pressure that move, make sounds, and play music.
1672	Baron Gottfreid Welhelm von Leibniz, a German philosopher/mathematician, invents a successful calculating machine.
1801	Joseph Jacquard, French silk-weaver and engineer, invents the punch card for patterns on mechanical looms.
1830s	Charles W. Babbage, an English mathematician, uses Jacquard's idea and tries to build a hand-operated, general-purpose "difference engine" that produces accurate math tables.
1890	Herman Hollerith uses punch-card calculators for the U.S. Census to count the population for the first time.
1904	Sir John Ambrose Fleming, British inventor, develops the diode vacuum tube that makes digital electronics possible.
1917	British military use vacuum tube calculators to crack German secret codes during World War I.
1936	Alan M. Turing, British mathematician, has the idea for a Universal Machine, paving the way for the general-purpose computer.
1943	Drs. Warren McCulloch and Walter Pitts create first artificial neural (brain nerve) connections and artificial cells.
1944	Mark I giant calculator, 52 feet (15.85 meters) long and 8 feet (2.44 meters) high, is developed at Harvard for World War II projects to develop the atomic bomb.
1945	ENIAC, with 19,000 vacuum tubes, becomes first programmable calculator. It weighs over 30 tons. EDVAC is first programmable computer with internal memory and programmable storage.

1948	Bell Laboratories invents the solid-state transistor, making the microprocessor possible years later. MADM is first chess-playing computer.
1950	Turing develops the Turing Test for artificial intelligence.
1956	Herbert Simon and Allan Newell develop Logic Theorist, first program to try to learn rules of human thinking process. John McCarthy coins the term "artificial intelligence."
1957	Simon and Newell invent the General Problem Solver along artificial intelligence principles.
1961	First industrial robot is installed by founders of Unimation, Inc.
1962	Arthur Samuel's checker-playing computer defeats a former state champion.
1967	MacHack chess program wins a state championship.
1971	Microprocessor is invented, launching personal computer revolution.
1977	Chess 4.5 chess program achieves expert level ranking.
1979	Hans Berliner's backgammon-playing robot "Gammonoid" defeats human world champion.
Early 1980s	Case-based reasoning (CBR) "intelligent" programs become useful.
1983	"Belle" is first chess program to achieve master ranking.
1986	Berliner's HiTech chess computer achieves international master ranking.
1989	Deep Thought chess computer loses to Gary Kasparov.
1990	Mephisto chess computer defeats Anatoly Karpov, former world champion.
1996	The IBM Deep Blue chess computer, "son" of Deep Thought, loses to Kasparov, current world champion.
1997	Deep Blue defeats Kasparov.

Glossary

Artificial intelligence (AI)—man-made ability to think and act like humans independently, without direct human involvement

Artificial life—branch of AI research that seeks to develop intelligent machines with the ability to "learn" as a situation changes and different processes interact

Biorobot—a behavior-based robot that works according to artificial life principles

Case-based reasoning (CBR)—a branch of rule-based AI through which computers "learn" to apply a new solution to a problem based on the circumstances of many similar past situations

Emotional intelligence—an AI method in which a computer uses natural language, voice recognition, and advanced algorithms to appear to recognize and respond to human emotions and appear to express its own humanlike conditions

Fuzzy logic—branch of computing and mathematics that uses probability and uncertainty principles to solve problems

Heuristics—AI method through which computers are programmed with the rules of how something works and applies those rules to solve problems

Intelligent assistant—AI application through which intelligent programs or machines carry out the functions of human workers

Machine learning—type of AI through which computers and machines "learn" by repeating actions and correcting mistakes

Machine vision—type of AI that uses pattern recognition software and sensors to "see" objects

Microelectromechanical machines (MEMS)—microscopic-sized machines with electrical and mechanical components, but without any AI ability

Natural language—in AI, a method through which computers are programmed to understand, learn from, and respond to normal human speech and writing

Neural networks—programmed integrated circuit chips that seek to duplicate how the human brain works through the interaction of neurons and synapses

Robot—an electromechanical machine with some humanlike intelligence programmed into its onboard computer

Softbot—software with artificial intelligence capability that executes tasks normally associated with human activity

Verbot—type of softbot that uses speech synthesis and voice recognition AI software to interact with people and carry out normal activities

Virtual personality—an AI program or machine that displays a humanlike appearance and speaks and acts in a humanlike manner

Voice recognition—capability of an AI program to decode actual human speech patterns through repetitive practice and natural language programs

To Find Out More

Books

Cochrane, Kerry. *The Internet*. New York: Franklin Watts, 1997.

Darling, David. J. *Computers of the Future: Intelligent Machines and Virtual Reality*. Morristown, NJ: Dillon Press, 1995.

Gershenfeld, Neil A. *When Things Start to Think*. New York: Henry Holt & Company, 1999.

Jefferis, David. *Artificial Intelligence: Robotics and Machine Evolution*. New York: Crabtree Publishing, 1999.

Jeunesse, Gallimard. *Inside Machines (Scholastic Voyages of Discovery, 21)*. New York: Scholastic Trade, 2000.

Lampton, Christopher. *The World Wide Web*. New York: Franklin Watts, 1997.

Leonard, Andrew. *Bots: The Origin of New Species*. New York: Penguin USA, 1998.

McNeil, Daniel, and Freiberger, Paul. *Fuzzy Logic: The Revolutionary Computer Technology That Is Changing Our World*. New York: Touchstone Books, 1994.

Stork, David. G. *HAL's Legacy: 2001's Computer as Dream and Reality*. Cambridge, MA: MIT Press, 1998.

Wickelgrean, Ingrid. *Ramblin' Robots: Building a Breed of Mechanical Beasts*. New York: Franklin Watts, 1997.

Online Sites

KidsClick
http://sunsite.berkeley.edu/KidsClick
A useful website with a powerful search engine managed by librarians.

The Kids Report
http://scout.cs.wisc.edu/scout/KIDS/current/index.html
The KIDS Report is a biweekly publication produced by K-12 students.

Newton's Apple
http://www.pbs.org/ktca/newtons/15/robots.html and
http://www.pbs.org/ktca/newtons/15/nasa.html
The first site summarizes a segment of the *Newton's Apple* public TV show that focused on robots. The second site summarizes a segment on how NASA uses robots for space exploration.

Planet K-12
http://planetk-12.planetsearch.com/
An easy, useful search engine helpful in finding materials related to school assignments.

A Science Fair Project Resource Guide
http://www.ipl.org/youth/projectguide/
An excellent resource from the Internet Public Library that links kids to resources for projects.

Study Web
http://www,studyweb.com/computers/ai.htm
Study Web is a huge site with thousands of links to every topic you ever need to study. The computer section has an AI division with hundreds of websites.

The Amazing Robot Museum
http://www.the-robotman.com/museum.html
This is the site of a museum dedicated to the history of robots with lots of information and pictures.

Cathy's Picnic

http://www.geocities.com/Heartland/7134/indexa.html

You'll find a fun site with an alien village project and dancing with disco robots.

Cool Robot of the Week

http://ranier.hq.nasa.gov/telerobotics_page/coolrobots.html

Here is a NASA site that leads to innovative sites devoted to robot development.

Design Your Own Robot

http://www.tcm.org/html/galleries/robots/design/using-des.html

Here is an interactive site that lets you design your own robot based on your mission; for example, search a sunken ship for treasure. Learn the six basic robotic functions.

Get a Grip on Robotics

http://www.thetech.org/hyper/robots/teaser/

A well-illustrated exhibit shows you a jointed-arm robot that looks and works almost like your arm—with one interesting exception.

Net-Robot

http://www.fh-konstanz.de/studium/ze/cim/projekte/webcam/

Here is an AI program in a game called Tower of Hanoi that pits you against an AI computer by moving discs between towers.

Tech Wizards
http://www.hompro.com/techkids/
This site focuses on how robots and electronics work, and how they are used. It provides resources and projects with links to websites around the world.

The Tech Museum of Innovation
http://www.thetech.org/
This is an educational resource with interesting exhibits about computers, satellites, robotics, lasers, and more.

The Telegarden.
http://www.usc.edu/dept/garden/
This tele-robotic installation allows WWW users to view and interact with a remote garden filled with living plants.

Xavier
http://www.cs.cmu.edu/People/Xavier/
You can command Xavier anytime, and see your commands carried out live when the robot is online.

A Note on Sources

Robots and artificial intelligence have fascinated everyone from children to scientists for more than 50 years. As you can see from my list of references, you can easily find hundreds of books, articles, websites, and learning resources on every aspect of AI. Most of the resources for children focus on robots because they are "cool" and children can play with them. To have fun, you should try the museum and game websites. For the book, I focused on sources for adults, starting with Jim Hogan's book *Mind Matters*, an excellent history of the development of AI. Then, I "surfed" the World Wide Web, finding many articles, websites for serious research programs, and commercial AI software companies. I found that although we may not yet have robotic maids that clean our homes, artificial intelligence will soon be everywhere in everything making our lives easier and more convenient.

Index

Numbers in *italics* indicate illustrations.

About the Author

Noted author Robert L. Perry has written about personal computers for more than 20 years. He wrote one of the first books about microcomputers for home use and has authored two other books about computers and computer-related careers for Franklin Watts, including *Computer Crime* and *Electronic Service Careers*. He teaches professional writing at the University of Maryland, College Park, has a master's degree in speech communication, and makes his home near Annapolis, Maryland.